find out what to do with your gold coins at the back of the book.

With special thanks to Tabitha Jones

For Aaron Simpkins

www.beastquest.co.uk

ORCHARD BOOKS

First published in Great Britain in 2019 by The Watts Publishing Group

1 3 5 7 9 10 8 6 4 2

Text © 2019 Beast Quest Limited.
Cover and inside illustrations by Steve Sims
© Beast Quest Limited 2019

Beast Quest is a registered trademark of Beast Quest Limited
Series created by Beast Quest Limited, London

A CIP catalogue record for this book is available from the British Library.

ISBN 978 1 40834 307 4

Printed in Great Britain

The paper and board used in this book are made from wood from responsible sources

Orchard Books
An imprint of Hachette Children's Group
Part of The Watts Publishing Group Limited
Carmelite House, 50 Victoria Embankment, London EC4Y 0DZ

An Hachette UK Company
www.hachette.co.uk
www.hachettechildrens.co.uk

SCALAMANX
THE FIERY FURY

BY ADAM BLADE

ORCHARD

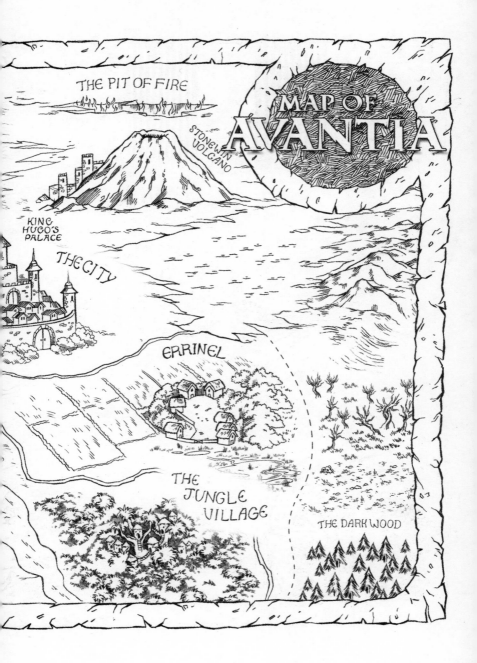

CONTENTS

STORY ONE

MAGIC THEFT

The Circle of Wizards always feared me. They called my magic unnatural, evil, forbidden. Those old crones and greybeards were just jealous of anyone with a mind of their own. That's why they expelled me all those years ago.

But I'm sure the young apprentices still whisper my name in awe behind their masters' backs.

I've been in hiding too long. It's time to pay my old foes a little visit. To strike them where it will hurt the most, by taking their greatest treasures. And when I'm done, and they scratch their ancient heads in confusion, I will be far away, laughing...

The Locksmith

A PLEA FOR HELP

Tom and Elenna stood together in the throne room, watching two of Captain Harkman's soldiers lift a new tapestry into place. A solemn hush filled the chamber, broken only by happy gurgles from baby Prince Thomas, sitting on Queen Aroha's lap. At the king's side, Captain Harkman and the wizard Daltec lowered their heads in respect. A mixture of awe and sorrow filled Tom.

The tapestry had been stitched by the finest artisans in Avantia. The bright embroidery showed Prince Angelo's final battle against Uthrain of the Wildlands, more than thirty years ago. Angelo, King Hugo's older brother, had defeated his enemy to end the long war between Avantia and the barbarians of the north…but not before receiving a fatal blow himself.

King Hugo let out a long sigh. "Now my brother's courage will never be forgotten," he said, his voice hoarse with emotion.

Tom's own throat tightened as he remembered gazing down into the prince's lonely grave in the Wildlands. He and Elenna had only recently returned from discovering where Angelo's body lay. Then, armed with the truth, they had defeated a shapeshifting Beast claiming to be the long-lost prince, returned to claim the throne.

"It's very lifelike," Elenna said, gazing up at the tapestry. The morning sun slanting through the throne room windows lit Angelo's strong features. Tom could see the grim determination in the wounded prince's gaze as he drove his opponent back. He found himself marvelling at the young warrior's strength and courage.

A squelchy hiccup broke Tom's train of thought. He looked down to see baby Thomas's round face peeking over the queen's shoulder, a string of milky drool hanging from his lip. Tom smiled. The prince grinned back at him, showing off his first tooth.

Aroha let out a theatrical sigh. "Oh, Thomas!" she said. "This is my best dress!" She scrubbed at a white stain on the silk with her handkerchief, then started patting the prince's back. With each gentle thud, Tom could hear more squidgy gurgles coming from the baby's throat. He edged back a little.

Suddenly a brilliant white flash lit the room, blinding Tom. The light faded to reveal two cloaked figures standing before the king and queen, one tall and straight, the other slight and bent over a staff.

"What evil magic is this?" Harkman

demanded, leaping forward, his sword raised. The pair scowled back at him. The shorter of the two, a woman with iron-grey hair, waved her hand. Harkman's sword instantly transformed, curling in on itself with a hiss to become a red and green snake

with yellow fangs.

"Gah!" Harkman threw the creature on to the flagstones, where it changed again into a tangle of silk scarves.

Elenna hurriedly aimed an arrow at the intruders, but Tom rested a hand on her arm.

"It's all right," he said. "We know these two." He dipped his head respectfully to the elderly woman – the head of the Circle of Wizards. "Sorella," he said, then he frowned at the slender man by her side. They had met before – Tom recognised the youth's thin-lipped sneer and pale eyes. He also remembered how badly the young wizard had treated Daltec. "I'm afraid I don't recall your name," Tom said.

A look of irritation flitted across the young man's face, quickly replaced by a smarmy smile as he bowed low to the king and queen. "My name is Stefan, your Majesties," he said. "Lawkeeper of the Circle of Magic."

"That's all very well," Captain Harkman said, "but it doesn't explain why you've appeared out of thin air before the king and queen with no prior appointment!"

Sorella sighed. "I do apologise for our sudden entrance," she said, "but we have come on a most pressing matter. We require your...assistance."

"Our assistance?" Hugo said. "It's not like the Circle to ask for help!"

Stefan shifted uncomfortably, his pale face flushing. "There has been

an…incident…" he said. "A theft. The day before yesterday, a large supply of magical ingredients and spell books went missing from our secure vault."

"Hmph. Not that secure then!" Harkman muttered. As Stefan glared at the captain, baby Thomas let out a shriek and squirmed to get down from Aroha's lap.

"Oh, go on then," Aroha said, setting Thomas on the floor. The prince crawled straight towards Stefan, who curled his lip in distaste.

"I take it that with all your magical powers you know who is responsible for the theft?" Aroha asked the intruders.

"Alas, no," Sorella said. "There is but one key to the vault, and Stefan wears it around his neck."

"It sounds like wizards' business to me," Aroha said.

"Unfortunately, this matter affects us all," Sorella told her. "Among the stolen items were several Beast artefacts. There is a very real risk to the kingdom if they fall into the wrong hands."

Tom exchanged a look of alarm with Elenna. But before either of them could question Sorella further, Tom heard a wet splat from Prince Thomas's direction. Stefan leaped away from the baby, his boots splattered with milky sick and face twisted with revulsion. *Good shot!* Tom thought. The prince squeaked with pleasure as Stefan flapped his robe and hopped from foot to foot.

Sorella shot Stefan a stern look, then turned her sharp gaze on Tom. "We are willing to repay you for your help in this matter," she said. "Young man, I have heard that you were recently stripped of your magical powers. Find our missing artefacts, and my colleagues and I will attempt to restore your shield tokens and the Golden Armour."

Tom's heart leaped. *With my powers back, I'd be able to defend the kingdom properly again!* But then he forced himself to take a measured breath. *The most urgent thing is to stop those Beast tokens falling into the wrong hands!*

Suddenly, baby Thomas let out an

excited squeal, reaching towards the
open window. Tom glanced up and
just caught a glimpse of a bright
red crow resting on the sill, before it
flapped its wings and flew away.

"Rourke!" Elenna said.

"Who?" Aroha said, frowning after the bird.

"Petra the witch's spy," Tom called back, already heading for the door. "Which means she's close!"

OUTNUMBERED

Time to make a speedy exit, Rourke!
Petra thought, as her bird swooped
from the window ledge above.

She darted out from behind a pile
of hay bales and ran towards the
stable door. After a quick glance
around the bustling city square, she
lowered her head and scurried out.

Shoppers stood gossiping in groups,
while merchants held up swathes of

cloth or colourful ornaments, shouting about their wares. Petra hurried between them towards the City's main gate.

"Stop her!" a familiar female voice suddenly shouted.

Elenna! Petra looked back to see the short-haired girl dashing through the

palace courtyard gates with Tom at her side, their weapons drawn.

With a flick of her fingers, Petra sent a basket of apples toppling from a merchant's cart and across their path. *Stay close, Rourke!* she told her pet as she hurried onwards through the crowd.

"Get her, quick!" someone cried from her left. A gangly squire with a skimpy beard grabbed her arm, but Petra hurled a fistful of magic into his chest, throwing him backwards. He landed on his rump with a startled cry. Petra couldn't help giggling at his outraged expression as she raced on.

With the gate in view, she grinned to herself. *They won't catch me now!* But then she heard the clatter of chains from ahead. A burly guard glared back at her from the gatehouse, hurriedly turning the winch to lower the portcullis. *Rourke, stop him!* Petra told her crow. The red bird dived at the man, flapping and pecking at his face, but the iron gate was already halfway down. Holding on to her hat,

Petra threw herself forward with a final burst of speed, skidding under the sharp points of the portcullis just before it slammed down with a clang. She turned to see Tom and Elenna pull up on the other side, red-faced and panting. *Ha ha! Too slow!*

"Why were you spying on us?" Elenna demanded.

Petra shrugged. "I just like to keep up to date with what's going on, that's all."

"You mean you stole from the Circle of Wizards and wanted to know if you'd been found out yet!" Elenna snapped.

Petra grinned. "You'll have to think harder than that if you want to help those old fuddy-duddies get their trinkets back!" Then she blew Tom a kiss and turned to race away.

She had barely run five paces when the air shimmered and two cloaked forms appeared in her path. *Sorella and Stefan! Stuck-up busybodies!*

"Hello!" she said, trying for a friendly smile. "And how can I help my fellow witches and wizards today?"

The old woman scowled. "You can give us back our stolen possessions," she said.

Petra held up her hands. "I didn't take anything!"

"You expect us to believe that?" Stefan said, scowling. "You've done it before. Remember the Lightning Staff incident?"

"But that was to stop an evil

sorceress in Henkrall," Petra said. "I'm
on your side!"

"Tell that to the Circle," Stefan said.
He stepped forward, lifting a hand
to cast a spell, but Petra grinned and

opened her own fist, showing him a small green vial.

"One more move and I'll turn you into a newt!" she said.

Stefan's mouth dropped open and he flushed red. Sorella looked so angry she might burst into flames. But before Petra could push past them, she heard a rattling clank from behind her. She spun to see the portcullis rise quickly, and Tom and Elenna stepped through.

"You're surrounded!" Tom said.

Not if I can help it! Petra snatched another vial from her pocket, this one blue, and smashed it on the ground. A crackling sound filled the air as Tom and Elenna froze in place. Petra turned to see Sorella and Stefan also as still as ice statues, both wearing the same furious scowls. She sketched them a quick bow, then turned away.

But, with her next step, Petra ran into something solid, like an invisible wall. *A force field!* She glanced over her shoulder to see Daltec standing on the battlements, his outstretched hands glowing with purple energy.

Petra let out a heavy sigh. *Rats!*

THE LOCKSMITH

Tom and Elenna followed Captain Harkman and Daltec into a cold, dank cell beneath the palace. Sorella and Stefan crowded in close behind them.

Petra sat with her back against the wall and her manacled hands in her lap. She turned and rolled her eyes. "What now?" she said.

"Now we should strip you of your

powers," Sorella said.

"That's something I'd like to see," Stefan said. "But first we need to get the truth out of her, don't you think?" Tom didn't like the spiteful tone in the young wizard's voice.

"I'm bored of all this questioning," Petra said. "As I told you before, I didn't steal anything. But if your security is so lax, maybe you deserved to get robbed."

Sorella let out a hiss and lifted her hands. Her palms started to glow blood-red as she stepped forward, looming over Petra. The young witch flinched, and Tom was about to step between them when Captain Harkman spoke up. "I won't allow torture!" he said.

"The witch is our problem, not yours,"

Stefan snapped.

"Not here, she isn't," Harkman said. "In Avantia, the king is responsible for justice."

Sorella turned on Harkman sharply, her hands fading back to their normal colour. "Then we shall speak to him at once!" she said, glaring. "Lead the way, Captain."

"Very well," said Harkman. "Follow me."

As soon as Sorella and Stefan had swept from the room, Petra started to snigger.

Tom felt a familiar wave of frustration wash over him. *Doesn't she ever take anything seriously?*

"I don't know what you're so pleased about!" Elenna said, echoing his thoughts. "King Hugo won't just let you go free if the Circle of Wizards can prove you've stolen from them."

"Then it's a good thing I didn't!" Petra said. But then her lips spread in a sly grin and she looked sideways up at Tom. "Although I might know who did…"

Tom waited, irritation growing inside him as Petra sat smiling to herself. "Well, tell us then!" he said at last. "If we catch the real thief, Sorella will have to let you go."

"Have you heard of a wizard who calls himself the Locksmith?" Petra asked.

"Vaguely," Daltec said. "But he disappeared years ago. I seem to remember him meddling with dangerous magic. He ended up paying the price."

"That's him!" Petra said. "He was a metallurgist and discovered a way to forge Apertium – a magical metal that he used to make keys that fit any lock, and which open portals into different worlds."

"Yes," Daltec said. "That's what got him into trouble. He vanished through one of those portals and didn't come back."

"Well, now he has," Petra said.

Elenna frowned thoughtfully. "I suppose having a magical key would explain how he got into the vault," she said.

"Oh, very good, Elenna," Petra said, her voice dripping with sarcasm. "Well done!"

"So where has he taken the loot?" Tom asked, before Elenna could respond.

A calculating look crept into Petra's eyes. "I tell you what," she said. "I'll do you a deal. You let me go…and then I'll show you how to find him."

Elenna laughed. "You expect us to believe you?" she said. "How about you tell us first and then we let you go?"

Petra cocked her head. "Surely after the number of times I've saved your skins you owe me a tiny bit of trust?"

Elenna still looked uncertain. Tom didn't feel that much like trusting Petra either, but it wasn't as if they had any other leads to follow. *And until we recover those Beast artefacts the whole kingdom is at risk!*

"Fine," he said. Then he slipped out of the room to fetch a key from the guard post. When he returned, Petra held her manacles out to him. As soon as the shackles hit the floor with a clang, Petra threw her arms around Tom, crushing him in a hug so sudden he didn't even struggle. When she finally let him go, Tom stepped back, his face flushing hot.

Elenna smiled and raised her eyebrows at him, but then her expression changed to alarm. "Sorella and Stefan are coming back!" she said. Sure enough, Tom could hear footsteps in the passage outside. He turned to Petra.

"Quick, show us where the Locksmith is!" he said. Without answering, Petra took a small bag from her pocket and started pouring black powder on the ground, making a circle. Then she stepped to the wall and removed the burning torch from its bracket.

"Hurry up!" Elenna said, just as the door burst open and Sorella and Stefan marched in.

Petra lowered the torch to the

powder on the floor. *Whoosh!* It went up immediately, hiding her behind a curtain of green flames. The fire burned out in an instant. But Petra was gone.

Tom felt sick as he gazed at the space where Petra had been standing. "She told us she'd lead us to the thief," he said.

"And you believed her?" Sorella cried. Then she turned on her heel. "Stefan – come! We have to tell the king of this at once!" Sorella cast a furious look back at Tom and Elenna, then swept from the room with Stefan hurrying after her.

"Petra really has sunk to new depths this time," Elenna said glumly as their footsteps died away.

Tom let out a sigh. "I suppose we had better go and explain to King Hugo," he said. As he turned to leave, Elenna grabbed his arm.

"Wait!" she said. "What's that in your belt?"

Tom felt around his waist and found a scroll tucked into the back.

4

SCARECROWS

The green flames surrounding Petra died, and bright sunlight flooded her vision. She shaded her eyes to see more green all around her – grass this time, covering a gently sloping hill. As she gazed out over the new landscape, a jolt of alarm fizzed through her. She could see about a dozen horned figures scattered through a cornfield below. Petra dropped to a crouch, her heart hammering in her chest. *What are they? Goblins?* The menacing forms, dressed in ragged clothing, seemed to be gazing back at her from dark eye sockets. But then Petra let out a snort of laughter.

Scarecrows! They looked like they

had been made from animal skulls and bones, clutching old scythes. *Creepy*, Petra thought. Thinking of crows, she hoped Rourke was doing all right in Avantia without her. She scanned the rest of her surroundings. Nestled between two low hills in the distance, she could see a small village of thatched houses. Nearer by, in the cornfield, the sails of a white windmill turned lazily.

Petra smiled to herself. *There's no wind today. So that must be a clue...* Her mother, Kapra, had once told her this was where the Locksmith grew up, so Petra had guessed he might be hiding here. *And it looks like I was right...*

She made her way down the

hill. At the bottom, she pushed through scratchy corn towards the whitewashed building. She found a donkey out front, feeding from a trough of oats, still roped to a covered wagon. *Looks like someone's at home,* Petra thought. *But I'd better hurry. Once Tom finds my map, he and Elenna won't be far behind.*

As Petra strolled past, the donkey looked up at her from dull brown eyes, then went back to its meal. Other than the steady chomping of its jaws and the creaking of the windmill's slow sails, the place was eerily quiet. Petra stood on tiptoe and tried peering through a latticed window, but sunlight reflected off the glass and it was too dim inside to see through.

Circling the windmill, she found a door with a shiny silver knocker in the shape of a dog's head. She rapped once, then waited. No answer. She put out her hand to rap again. As her fingers touched the knocker, its snout wrinkled back, showing shiny teeth.

"What do you want?" the knocker snarled.

"I want to speak with your master," Petra said. "I am an enemy of the Circle of Wizards and I've come to make a trade."

The dog's head narrowed its eyes, watching her with distrust, but then the door swung open. Petra stepped through to find herself in a dusty, cluttered room. The rich, savoury smell of cooking hung in the air, making Petra feel suddenly hungry. Not much light made it through the grimy windows, and a bubbling pot covered most of a fire in one corner. In the dimness Petra could just make out rows of shelves stacked with bottles, bones and other artefacts.

Near the fire, a squat man sat at a desk covered with open books and scrolls. He wore a brown robe and his bald head and long, plaited beard made Petra think of a monk.

"I've come to do a deal," Petra said.

With a sigh, the man looked up, irritation written across his plump face as he fixed her with shrewd, dark eyes. "I've just furnished myself with the entire contents of the Circle of Wizards' secret vault," he said. "What

could you possibly have that I need?"

Petra hitched her chin. "I'm Kapra's daughter," she said, lifting her small sack. "I have the only thing you desire. Apertium."

The man narrowed his eyes doubtfully, but Petra could see the hungry interest in his gaze. She felt the first warm tingle of triumph. *He's going to take the bait...*

"Apertium is very rare," the Locksmith said. "I expect you've found Xorium or some other lesser metal."

Petra smiled to herself. *No metal at all in fact, only a forgery spell...*

She pulled one of her counterfeit coins from her bag and flicked it to him. He caught it with a pudgy hand, then fitted a jeweller's eyeglass to his eye. Petra watched, her palms getting sweatier by the moment as the little man inspected the coin. He bit it, and even took a long sniff of the metal.

Finally, the Locksmith closed his hand around the coin, and nodded to her. "How much do you have?" he asked her.

"Fifty coins, just like that one," Petra said. "So, what can I get?"

"For fifty coins, you can choose what you like," he said. "I've got invisibility potions, a time-travel sundial, animation fluids…" He heaved himself up and crossed to a shelf, plucking a vial from the mess. As he tilted it, a purple liquid swirled about inside. "This is the last of my Floating Elixir. Now that the wells on Makai are dry, you're unlikely to find more anywhere else."

"Hmm…I don't know," Petra said, pretending to think. The Locksmith set the vial back on its shelf and picked up a small metal case. Back

at his desk, he opened the box with
a flourish. Petra stepped closer and
found an assortment of metal keys of
different shapes and sizes inside.

"These are made of Apertium," the
man said. "With the right key, you can
go to any kingdom – anywhere!"

"Hmm," Petra said. "I guess
that could be useful. But there is
something else I was thinking of."
Petra almost couldn't bring herself
to say the words – but she swallowed
her embarrassment and went on. "Do
you have any love potions?" she asked.

He gaped at her. "A love potion! Is
that all?" Then he smiled. "I suppose
I might have one left," he said. He
rummaged in a drawer beneath his
desk, and eventually pulled out a

small vial. "Here you go," he said. "Put this in a drink, and the drinker will fall madly in love with the first person they see."

Petra took the vial and slipped it

into her cloak pocket, almost grinning at the thought of all the mischief she would cause.

"So, who's the lucky boy?" the Locksmith said.

Petra felt her face flush hot, which surprised her. "None of your business!" she snapped. Then she dropped her bag on the desk. It made a soft thump instead of the metallic clunk of coins that it should have. *Uh-oh. My spell's failed!*

"Goodbye," she said as cheerily as she could, backing towards the door. The Locksmith frowned down at the bag, then snatched it up and tipped it. Sand trickled out. Petra spun and sprinted from the room, hearing the small man roar with fury behind her.

She raced into the cornfield, then skidded to a stop. *Uh-oh!* Every one of the hideous scarecrows had turned to face her, showing their wide, grinning mouths. All at once, they lurched forward.

"No one cheats me!" the Locksmith bellowed from the windmill behind her. Petra swallowed as the scarecrows closed in on her, brandishing their rusty scythes.

5

THE LOCKSMITH'S WINDMILL

Tom felt a jolt as his stallion Storm's hooves thudded down on to solid ground. The rushing wind of Daltec's magic subsided and the swirling colours before Tom's eyes settled into green grass and blue sky.

"I don't see any buildings," Elenna said from the saddle behind him. "Where are we?" Tom unrolled Petra's map and scanned it. Glancing back over his shoulder, he could see a copse of trees and more distant hills. Ahead, a grassy slope banked gently upwards.

"It looks like we've arrived just inside Rion," Tom said, pointing to a spot on the map. "This hill will lead us into a shallow valley. The Locksmith's house should be somewhere below." Tom kicked Storm into a canter, and soon reached the top of the hill. As he slowed his horse, he could hear strange crackles and bangs coming from below. He shaded his eyes and saw a windmill ahead, in the middle of a cornfield. Near the building, a group of tall, horned figures surrounded a smaller cloaked form, whose hands crackled with blue light.

"Petra!" Tom's pulse quickened as he saw the glint of blades in the taller figures' hands. *She's in trouble!*

Tom urged Storm down the slope. As they drew nearer, he noticed the gangly creatures had sheep's skulls for heads. *Living scarecrows!* he realised, with a jab of horror. As soon as Storm came within range, Elenna loosed an arrow. It flew past Tom and struck the creature closest to Petra, just as the witch hurled a ball of silvery flames that sent it toppling backwards. It hit the ground with a clatter and tumbled apart, suddenly just a pile of rags and bones. But Petra was still badly outnumbered.

Tom halted Storm and leaped down, closely followed by Elenna.

He raced forward and swung for Petra's nearest attacker from behind. His sword met barely any resistance at all, slicing the vile creature in half. It collapsed to the ground and fell apart, its skull rolling away. Using her bow like a staff, Elenna swiped the grinning head off another scarecrow.

Two of the monsters lurched at Tom, fixing him with empty eye sockets. As he hacked at one, the other swung its scythe for his chest, but he spun and caught it with a backhanded stroke, sending it crashing to the ground. He glanced about quickly and saw that Petra and Elenna had finished off the other scarecrows, although the witch had a bleeding wound on her arm.

"Are you all right?" Tom asked as

she rubbed some salve on the cut. It stopped bleeding at once, but still looked angry and sore.

"I'll live," she said. "Thanks to you two."

"Hmph," Elenna said. "What were you doing here anyway?"

"I thought I'd give you a hand, and try and capture the Locksmith," Petra said, blushing. "He lives in that windmill over there." She pointed.

"You've done your part by giving us the map," Tom said. "We'll take it from here." He strode towards the windmill, pushing through the broken cornstalks and giving the fallen scarecrows a wide berth. Petra and Elenna kept pace behind him.

"Be careful," Petra said, as they

approached. "That door-knocker is made of Apertium. It has a nasty bite."

"That's right!" the dog's-head knocker snarled, suddenly coming to life. "Knock and I'll have your fingers!"

Tom shrugged, then drew back his foot and kicked the door. It burst open, revealing a plump and balding man standing behind a desk. He looked up, fury contorting his face, and snapped shut the metal box he held.

Tom stepped through the entrance, his sword raised. Beside him, Elenna aimed her bow.

"It's over," Tom said. "You must face the Circle of Wizards and answer for your crimes."

The Locksmith snorted. "I don't think so," he said. "They're nothing but a bunch of liars and thieves. I refuse to play by their rules." He snatched up the box from the table.

Elenna fired her arrow. It slammed into the box, knocking it from the Locksmith's hand and sending a shower of metal keys clattering on to the desk. The Locksmith grabbed one and turned to a door behind him. Tom dived around the desk, but already the small man had the door open and was slipping through. Tom caught a glimpse of almost painfully bright green foliage and shimmering purple flowers, before the door slammed shut in his face. *Gwildor! But... But how? We're in Rion!*

Tom threw the door open again, ready to dash into his mother's

homeland, but he only found dusty overalls hanging from a peg beside a few brushes and brooms. *A cupboard!*

Tom let out a growl of frustration. *He's escaped!*

6

MISCHIEF AND MAYHEM

Petra watched as Tom carefully collected up the Locksmith's fallen keys and put them back in their box. He handled them gingerly, as if they might suddenly whisk him away to another kingdom.

"He's a slippery one," Petra said, leaning against the doorframe. "I doubt you'll catch him now."

Tom held up one of the keys. "Can't we use one of these?" he asked. "You said they fit into any lock."

Petra shook her head. "Yes, but each key leads somewhere different and I have no idea how to tell where."

Elenna pushed past her from outside. "Instead of just standing in the way, can't you help me load all this stuff on to the cart, so we can return it?" she said, gesturing at the Locksmith's plunder.

Petra shrugged. "I suppose," she said. Then an idea struck her. "But first, why don't we eat? I'm starving, and that stew smells delicious. It's a shame to waste it and the Locksmith won't be needing it now."

"We can eat when we've finished

work," Tom said. He took a jar from a shelf and peered through the glass. There was a tuft of orange fur inside. "*Hair of Momax*?" Tom said, reading the label. "What is that anyway?"

"It's probably from a Beast," Petra said. "The old Masters of Beasts used

to give their tokens to the Circle of Wizards for safekeeping. Which, it turns out, was a big mistake…"

Tom picked up another jar. "*Fang of Scalamanx*," he read. "I think my mother fought him once. Some sort of lizard Beast."

"Well, it's a good thing the Locksmith doesn't have the Beast tokens any more," Elenna said, loading more jars into a box. "If he can bring scarecrows to life, he has to be pretty powerful."

Petra shrugged. "It's not that impressive." She crossed to a shelf and plucked two vials of blue liquid from a rack. "This stuff's animation fluid," she said. She started juggling the vials from hand to hand. "Just one drop is enough to bring anything to life – tables, chairs…anything."

"Don't spill any, then," Elenna snapped. She snatched one of the vials from the air, then held out her hand for the other.

Petra gave it to her with a sigh. "Some people have no sense of fun at all," she said.

With nothing better to do, Petra set to work stacking jars and artefacts into crates with Elenna, while Tom checked each item off on the Locksmith's ledger. Before long, the covered wagon was fully loaded with everything the Locksmith had stolen, plus most of his own potions, powders and keys.

Once Tom and Elenna were both

busy outside checking the donkey's harness, Petra grinned to herself. *Now for some fun!* She rummaged in the cupboard near the fire and found three dishes. After filling each with steaming stew, she glanced towards the door, then tipped the Locksmith's

love potion into one of the portions. Wearing her most innocent smile, she took up the bowls, carefully balancing two on one arm, and headed for the door.

Outside, Tom and Elenna had finished work. Tom took a swig from his water flask, then smiled at her. "Thanks for your help with this," he said. "When we've eaten, Elenna and I can head back to Avantia and clear your name."

"Sounds good to me," Petra said, handing Tom the bowl she'd added her potion to. Then she gave another bowl to Elenna and sat down with her back to the wall of the windmill to eat her own. Tom sat down too, and Petra watched, glee bubbling up inside her as he hungrily tucked into his stew.

"Mmm. This is good," he said. "But spicy!"

"I expect the Locksmith learned new recipes with all his travelling to different kingdoms," Petra said, hoping Tom would look up at her at any moment. As she took a small mouthful of stew, a wasp buzzed in front of her face. Petra batted it away, but it came straight back. She stood up to swat at the insect.

"I only hope it doesn't have any magical properties, given who made it," Elenna said.

"He'd hardly poison his own dinner," Tom answered. He had put down his spoon and was staring at

Elenna. She gazed back at him with a puzzled frown.

"Umm. Are you all right, Tom?" Elenna asked.

Tom grinned broadly and let out a sigh. "Never better," he said. "I just… I was wondering if you'd done your hair differently or something. It really suits you like that."

Elenna frowned. "Tom, are you sure you're all right?"

"Of course," he said, still staring at Elenna, a goofy smile plastered across his face. "I'm always happy when I'm on a Quest with a friend." Suddenly, Petra realised what Tom's daft expression meant.

The potion's made him fall for the wrong person! But then she noticed

Elenna gaping in confusion as Tom grinned back at her, and couldn't help smirking.

The wasp veered back, criss-crossing before Petra's face. *It's your fault my plan went wrong!* she thought, giving it a good swipe. The wasp shot sideways and stung the donkey's rump. Suddenly, the animal let out a whinny and reared up on its hind legs. The cart jerked, and Petra heard boxes falling inside and the tinkle of broken glass. The donkey came back down on to all fours and stood swishing its tail.

"Great!" Elenna grumbled. "Now we'll have to repack all the boxes!"

"Don't worry – I'll do it," Tom said, brightly. He started towards the wagon, but then froze as the whole cart began to tremble. *Uh-oh... Petra thought.* The donkey rolled its eyes as the canvas covering the wagon started to stretch and bulge. It looked as if something huge inside was growing bigger and bigger, pushing against the fabric. Tom grabbed Elenna and thrust her behind him as the wagon cover started to smoke and char around the edges.

Petra scrambled to her feet. *This does not look good...* A moment later, the whole canvas caught light, burning through to reveal a massive dark shape inside. Petra thought of all the Beast artefacts and flasks of animation fluid the Locksmith had stolen. *Not good at all...*

SCALAMANX

"Elenna, stay back!" Tom cried, his heart filled with terror for his friend. He threw his shield up before her, watching the bulging wagon cover burn to ash. Something huge and black clambered from beneath the flaming canvas and on to the ground. It was a monstrous, reptilian creature like a giant lizard. Fiery tendrils surrounded its flat, blunt-nosed head, snaking about like whips. Dull black scales covered its sinuous body and glimmers of orange showed between the plates, like lava beneath a crust of rock. It turned to glare at Tom, from eyes like pits of fire.

"What is that?" Petra asked.

Tom took in the Beast's blazing eyes and the flaming whips cracking around its head. "Scalamanx!" he said, half remembering a story of one of his mother's Quests.

The donkey whinnied again, tossing its head as it struggled against its harness. Tom sprang forward and slashed through the leather straps, then leaped back to defend Elenna. The donkey bolted. At the same moment, Scalamanx started towards

Tom and his friends, each heavy footstep shaking the ground, leaving a burned, blackened mark. Tom lifted his sword and shield, and hunkered down, ready to fight. Just then, the Beast opened its vast jaws wide, and roared, blasting Tom with hot and noxious gasses that made his eyes water and his head spin.

As Tom shook his head to clear his senses, an arrow whizzed past him. It clattered off the Beast's stony scales, but Tom felt a rush of admiration for his friend. *Elenna truly is fearless!* Scalamanx lifted its head and let out another furious roar. The air shimmered with heat, and Tom could feel the hilt of his sword turning slippery with sweat. He tightened his grip, swallowing to try and wet his parched throat. Another arrow shot past him, this one lodging in the glimmering orange seam between two of the Beast's scales.

"Good shot!" Tom cried as the Beast recoiled with a furious hiss. Elenna fired another arrow, then another, filling Tom with awe as each shot bit deep into the Beast's hide.

Scalamanx backed away towards the windmill and started to climb, leaving a trail of soot on the whitewashed wall and making the building shake. But before Tom could begin to hope they had injured the Beast, Scalamanx turned to gaze down at them, its orange eyes burning brighter than ever.

The arrows lodged in Scalamanx's flesh charred to ash and crumbled away. At the same moment, the tendrils of flame surrounding its head licked upwards, catching the sails of the windmill. *Whoomph!* The four sails all went up at once, making Tom gasp. He stepped back, raising his shield before Elenna as great sheets of orange flame shot skywards.

"Come down here and fight!" he called to the huge salamander, all the while wracking his brains, trying to remember how his mother had beaten the creature. *It must have a weak spot... But right now, I can't see one.*

Petra leaped to his side and lifted her hands, firing two sizzling energy bolts towards the upper storeys of the

windmill. They hit with terrific cracks, splitting the brickwork and sending chunks of stone and burning wood clattering down around Scalamanx. The masonry tumbled off the creature's black scales, but it didn't even blink.

"Bring the whole building down!" Elenna told Petra.

"Good idea!" Tom said, impressed by Elenna's quick thinking. Petra lifted her hands again, hurling energy bolts so fierce they rocked the ground, throwing Tom to his knees. Dust and smoke filled the air and flying chips of stone stung his face. He leaped up and turned. *Where's Elenna?*

He found his companion scrambling to her feet, covered in dust. "Are you all right?" he asked.

"Don't worry about me," Elenna said, frowning past him. "Is the Beast dead?"

Tom glanced back to see a mound of smouldering debris where the windmill had been. But already the rubble was stirring. As he watched, the Beast's huge, blunt snout pushed up from the ruins. Scalamanx's eyes blazed as it clambered free and let out a furious hiss, the flaming tendrils around its head lashing wildly. Then, with a flick of its massive tail, the Beast sent a deadly barrage of fallen stone hurtling their way. *No!* Tom threw himself before his friend and braced himself behind his shield as the rubble hit. Every thud of stone

on wood jolted Tom's body, but he couldn't let anything harm Elenna.

When, at last, the dust settled, Tom saw Scalamanx retreating, leaving a path of scorched and smoking earth as it slunk off through the cornfield.

"Where is it going?" Elenna said.

"Probably to the village," Petra said. "There's one just between those hills."

Tom's stomach tightened with dread. "We have to stop it!" Lifting his hand to his mouth, he whistled for Storm. As the stallion drew to a halt before them, Tom offered Elenna his hand, but she leaped gracefully on to Storm's back without help. Tom felt an unfamiliar flutter in his chest as he swung up into the saddle too.

"What about me?" Petra called up from the ground.

But there was no time to spare. *We must defeat the Beast before it harms any innocent people!*

STORY TWO

THE RAGE OF SCALAMANX

Meddling witches I can deal with, but the boy with the sword and his pesky friend caught me by surprise. I should have known – Tom's reputation has spread across all the kingdoms I've visited. I've met many a Master of the Beasts in my time, great warriors with the strength of ten men, battle-scarred and brave. It's hard to see how this young lad has lasted so long.

Maybe his run of luck is coming to an end.

I will steer clear of Avantia and Rion for a few more years. Wait until all this is over. It would be a surprise if anyone survived the chaos to come...

The Locksmith

NEW PLANS

Petra gazed at the smoking ruins of the windmill, charred scraps of sailcloth falling like black snow all around her. The windmill's door still stood undamaged, complete with its shiny dog's-head knocker. But not much else.

Well, that didn't exactly go as planned... she thought, kicking a chunk of brick. *So, what now?* She briefly considered following Tom and Elenna. But chasing after a rampaging lava Beast didn't seem like much fun. And neither did watching Tom dote on Elenna like a lovesick puppy. *I should probably just lie low anyway*, she thought. *After all, I am a fugitive. Again.*

She picked her way towards the Locksmith's cart. Without its cover, she could see the boxes inside had all fallen from their neat piles and lay jumbled together. But they mostly seemed undamaged. And though the wood of the cart had charred in places it still looked roadworthy enough. She clambered up and peered into a fallen crate to see that only a couple of jars had broken, but then her gaze rested on the Locksmith's little box of keys. She grinned to herself. *I think a holiday's in order. I'll find a nice tropical island...*

Petra jumped off the cart, taking the small box with her, then she crossed to the wreckage of the windmill. Most of the brickwork surrounding the door had fallen away, and behind it lay nothing but ruins. *But it should still work...*

Petra rummaged in the box, running her hands over the keys, trying to see if she could get any clues where they might lead. But they all felt the same. She picked one at random and slotted the key into the door lock.

"What do you think you're doing?" the door-knocker barked. Petra ignored it and pushed the door open. Harsh

white light stung her eyes. She threw up a hand to shade them, and found herself looking down a steep rocky slope scattered with boulders and scree. Bright sun glinted off the pale, barren rock. Buzzards circled in the distance, letting out mournful cries. She couldn't see any other birds or plants, and definitely no beach. She shut the door again and picked a different key.

"You'll never find what you're looking for," the door-knocker said, smugly.

"If I wanted your opinion, I'd ask for it!" Petra said, then turned her new key in the lock. As she opened the door, an icy wind nearly tore the handle from her grip. It howled in her ears and snatched at her hair, scouring her face with sharp crystals of snow. Petra quickly slammed the door.

"Told you," the knocker said. Petra tried another couple of keys, but only managed to discover a very active-looking volcano, and a stinking bog with slimy black creatures like giant leeches squirming around in it. *Why would the Locksmith even bother making keys to places like that?* she wondered, shutting the box with a sigh.

Gazing about, Petra spotted the Locksmith's donkey chomping at some grass near the edge of the cornfield. Her spirits lifted at once. *I know! I'll take the cart and travel the kingdom. I'll sell off all the Circle's precious artefacts! Setting so much magic loose in one go should keep them busy, giving me the perfect opportunity to make some mischief of my own!*

Petra took a dried apple from her cloak pocket. Then she crept towards the donkey, making soft clicking sounds with her tongue. As the donkey looked up, Petra held out the apple.

The donkey's ears pricked, and Petra stepped closer, until she could hold the apple right beneath the donkey's nose. As the donkey nibbled the treat, Petra took hold of the animal's broken reins and led it back to its trough of oats. Now the Beast had gone, the donkey seemed happy enough munching quietly while she tied the straps together and hitched it to the cart.

Once the donkey was securely fastened, Petra climbed up into the back of the wagon and began tidying up her plunder. She quickly spotted something which made her grin. *A flask of Floating Elixir. Oh, this is too good an opportunity to miss!* she thought.

Petra dropped back to the ground. Then she sprinkled a few drops of elixir on each of the donkey's hooves. The animal let out panicked snorts as, one by one, its feet lifted off the ground. *It's working!* Petra stroked the creature's mane until it seemed calm. Then she poured some more of the potion on to the cart's wheels

and axles. The whole thing gave a
creaking lurch and bobbed up off
the ground. Petra let out a whoop.
Rourke's going to love this, she
thought. Then she climbed up into
the cart and took the reins, giving

them a sharp tug. The donkey lurched upwards. "Woo-hoo!" Petra cried as the charred remains of the windmill fell away below her.

Before long, the fields and woods looked like patches in a quilt. As her gaze fell on the black, scorched line that marked the path Scalamanx had taken towards the village, she felt a pang of guilt. *I wonder how Tom's getting on with that Beast?* But then she shrugged and focussed on the way the fresh, cool wind rushed through her hair and filled her lungs. *He'll be fine*, she told herself. *He's Master of the Beasts, after all!*

2

TRAPPED!

With Elenna seated behind him, Tom urged Storm onwards, filled with dread at the thought of carrying his dear friend into danger. *But I'll need her bravery and sharp shooting to have any hope of defeating Scalamanx.* A broad path of scorched stubble led away before them, right to the edge of the village. Even from a distance Tom could hear desperate shouts and

screams. *I hope we're not too late!*

   As they drew closer, Tom saw
plumes of smoke pouring into the
sky. Suddenly the sound of frenzied

hoofbeats filled the air. A flock of sheep clattered past so close, Storm reared up in surprise, and Tom almost lost his grip on the reins. He managed to bring Storm's hooves back to the ground only to see more stray animals tearing around, their eyes rolling in panic, and dark, smoking patches in their coats.

Before long, Tom and Elenna reached an outlying farm to find all the fences smashed or burned and the animals gone. A barn blazed nearby while farmhands raced back and forth from a well with buckets of water. One man with a sweat-streaked, sooty face turned to Tom and Elenna as they neared.

"There's a monster in the village

square!" he called. "The townsfolk are all fleeing for the hills. You should do the same if you value your skins."

"We're here to help," Elenna said.

"Get anyone you can to safety," Tom told the man. "We'll defeat the Beast." He tried to sound sure, though his gut twisted with fear at facing Scalamanx without his magical powers.

When they reached the first few cottages, a terrified scream ripped through the air. Tom pulled Storm to a halt and they dismounted, sprinting towards the frantic shouts. As they tore around a corner into the village square Tom saw the Beast bearing down on an elderly woman and a boy about his own age who wielded a plank of wood like a club. Scalamanx slunk closer, the lava veins in its flesh glimmering bright and its fiery tentacles thrashing.

Tom charged into the square, just as one of the Beast's fiery tendrils lashed forward and slapped the plank out of the boy's hand.

The two villagers cowered. Tom could see the boy trying to shield the old woman with his body though his eyes were wide with fear. Tom lifted his sword and lunged just as Scalamanx snapped its jaws at the villagers. With a double-handed blow Tom drove his blade between two stony plates on Scalamanx's tail, pinning it to the ground. The Beast's jaws clashed together, just a hand's breadth from the

boy's terrified face. With a furious snarl,
Scalamanx turned its blazing eyes on
Tom.

"Run!" Elenna shouted to the

villagers. "Get to safety while you can!" Her words seemed to free the pair from their terrified trance. The boy grabbed the woman by the hand and tugged her away.

Scalamanx roared, wrenching its tail free, leaving the tip still pinned to the ground by Tom's sword. With a glimmer of orange lava, the end of Scalamanx's tail regrew, while the severed tip crumbled to ash.

One of Elenna's arrows thudded into the lizard's side, but quickly burned away. Fear and frustration gripped hold of Tom as the Beast closed in on him. *If none of our weapons harm Scalamanx, how can we win?* Suddenly the fiery tentacles surrounding Scalamanx's head all lashed forward at once.

Tom threw up his shield. The burning tendrils clamped around it. Right away he realised his mistake. Without the protection of Ferno's dragon scale, his shield was nothing more than painted wood. It started to smoke and char. Still, it was the only protection Tom had. He held tight to the handle, but Scalamanx yanked with its crackling tentacles, sending Tom tumbling across the courtyard, his burning shield still clutched in his grip. He smashed shoulder-first though a wooden door and into a barn.

Winded and bruised, Tom glanced hurriedly about. In the dimness, he spotted a water trough. He rushed forward and plunged in his flaming shield. Steam hissed as the fire died, but Tom could already hear the heavy tread of the Beast behind him. He turned to see Scalamanx thrust its head into the barn. The orange glow from the Beast's eyes and tentacles threw up flickering shadows in the gloom. From the doorway, Elenna shot arrow after arrow, but Scalamanx didn't slow.

As the Beast neared, a wave of searing heat washed over Tom. He glanced about looking for anything he could use as a weapon but apart from a few bales of hay already starting to smoulder, the barn was empty. Scalamanx opened its vast jaws and roared, the rush of heat and fumes making Tom dizzy. He grabbed the side of the trough and pushed it over. Water sloshed across the floor, clouds of steam hissing upwards as it reached the salamander's feet. To Tom's surprise, the Beast let out a shriek and veered back, as if in pain. Scalamanx's

head whipped about in agony, the
water bubbling where it touched its
flesh.

So, the Beast does have a weakness!

"Elenna! Fetch water!" Tom
shouted. "As much as you can!" He
saw her hesitate for a moment in
the doorway, then turn and run. His
heart ached at the thought she might
be harmed, but he tore his eyes from
where she had been standing. The
Beast still bucked and writhed. Tom
took his chance. Dizzy with smoke
and heat, he dived past the wounded
creature and out of the barn.

Sucking in great gulps of fresh air,
Tom raced towards his sword and
yanked it from the ground. He turned
to see Scalamanx already lumbering

out into the open. The Beast lifted its massive tail and brought it crashing down.

The impact made the ground leap, throwing Tom from his feet. He hit the cobbles and started to scramble up, but one of the Beast's flaming tentacles whipped towards him, catching his ankle. *Argh!* Agony seared through him as his clothes burned, then his flesh. Tom gasped, breathless with pain as the Beast tugged. He hit the ground once more. Flames filled his vision as the Beast's fiery whips snaked towards him. He hacked with his sword at the fiery loop snagging his ankle and managed to cut himself free.

Tom staggered up, and started to

run, but his burned leg buckled. He staggered on a few desperate steps, only to feel fiery lashes strike his back, smashing him to the ground once again. He managed somehow to roll over and face the Beast, but then felt his last dregs of hope drain away. Scalamanx loomed above him, blasting his body with searing heat.

There's no way out!

3

TO THE RESCUE!

Petra smiled as the donkey tossed its head proudly, its hooves wheeling in the air as it pulled the wagon through the sky. *This beats walking any day!* In the cornfields below her, the dark pathway of the Beast was clearly visible. Ahead, Petra noticed plumes of smoke, rising into the sky. *Hmm. That doesn't look great*, she thought. She kept telling herself Tom would be fine. *He defeats Beasts all the time*... But something made her tug on the reins, angling their flight down towards the village.

As Petra drew closer to the ground, she frowned. Fires seemed to have sprouted all over the place, and a line of people carrying pails had formed between the village square and a duckpond nearby. Elenna stood by the pond, shouting orders and pointing.

Where's Tom? Petra asked herself. *Shouldn't he be doing his "While there's blood in my veins" speech by now?* As she neared the village square, she spotted the huge lava Beast they had awakened prowling about. Her heart gave a jolt. Right

before the fiery Beast lay a small,
defenceless figure – a boy. And he
wasn't moving. *Tom!* she realised.

Why isn't he fighting?

Petra bit her lip. *It's his own fault, really. He insists on battling monsters all the time when he knows Masters of Beasts usually die horribly...*

Still, in her heart, she knew she couldn't leave him. *It looks like it's down to me to come to the rescue – again!* She cracked the reins. The donkey let out a whinny of alarm but picked up its pace, diving lower. A sudden wave of heat and fumes hit Petra. She could hear the panicked shouts of the villagers clearly, and she saw the look of hopeless terror on Tom's face. The bottom of one of his trouser legs had charred away, showing a nasty red and black burn. Petra found herself craning forward, a horrible feeling squeezing her chest.

"I'm coming, Tom!" she shouted. Then she reached behind her, sought out a green vial from a box, and hurled it.

The vial broke right beside Tom, sending up a puff of smoke. When it cleared, Tom had vanished. *It worked! He's invisible!* Petra grinned as the Beast's flat head darted left and right, staring about in fury. Then it let out a howl of rage. *Ha ha! What are you going to do now?* But then Scalamanx looked up, its fiery eyes locking right on to Petra.

Time to go! she thought, tugging her reins one more. But as the cart lifted, one of the Beast's fiery tentacles reached out, wrapping around one

of the wheels. The wagon lurched
and the donkey snorted in panic, its
four hooves circling madly. Petra's
stomach flipped as they lost height
fast. *We're going down!* She braced
herself as the cobbles seemed to

rush up to meet her. With a crunch
of splintering wood, she felt the
reins torn from her hands as she flew
from her seat. Then the hard ground
punched the breath from her body.

She lay, winded and dazed, blinking
up at the sky. *I'm not dead!* She
heaved herself over to see Scalamanx
prowling towards her. She let out a
curse. *Spoke too soon!*

Petra tried to scramble up, but her
feet tangled in her cloak. As a wave
of fear hit her, she felt a firm hand on
her arm, pulling her to her feet. An
invisible hand.

"Where's Elenna?" Tom asked
urgently, his voice a pained croak
close to her ear. "I couldn't...bear it if
anything...happened to her!"

"We've got bigger problems right now!" Petra said, grabbing the invisible hand on her arm and tugging Tom back from the advancing Beast, a mass of crackling flames and snapping teeth. Petra glanced over her shoulder and her stomach dropped. With a building right behind her, there was nowhere else to go. Her mind raced, trying to think of a spell that might help. But at that moment, a crowd of villagers carrying buckets burst into the square, with Elenna in the lead.

"Please be careful, Elenna!" Tom cried. He struggled in Petra's grip, but she held him fast.

"Elenna can look after herself!" Petra said.

Water slopped from Elenna's bucket as she ran up behind the Beast then flung what remained over it. A cloud of steam went up with a hiss. Scalamanx's head snapped round, and it let out a growl as it spotted the villagers.

A tall young man with a soot-streaked face flung more water over the lava Beast. Then a slender woman with fierce dark eyes did the same. The Beast yelped as if it had been scalded, its whole body shuddering with agony. Bucket after bucket drenched the monster's flanks and the blistering heat in the square faded a little. Petra saw the glimmering lava beneath the Beast's skin dim, as if it was hardening to rock.

The snaking tendrils around
Scalamanx's neck flickered and
dwindled like guttering torches. As
another bucket of water sloshed over
its back, the Beast tossed its head,
turned and darted away. The villagers

scattered as the Beast charged
through their ranks and smashed
into the doors of a barn, disappearing
inside. Elenna reached Petra in an
instant.

"Where's Tom?" she asked.

"I'm right here," Tom said. "Elenna, you were amazing! I've never seen anything like it!"

Petra rolled her eyes. "I'm fine, thanks for asking!" she said, but when she saw Elenna's panic and confusion as she scanned the empty air, she sighed. "I just turned him invisible," she explained. "The spell will wear off eventually, but I can probably find something to reverse it quicker." The cart lay on its side not far from where she stood, though the donkey seemed to have floated away. *Well, at least someone's safe!* Petra crossed to the wagon's scattered contents with Elenna at her side. She selected another flask – this one orange – and held it out.

"This is a reversal potion," she said. "Tom? Are you there?"

"Yes," he said, from right beside Elenna. Petra rolled her eyes. *Of course – I should have guessed he wouldn't be far from his beloved!*

"Drink some of this, and you'll be visible again," Petra said. She felt a hand close over the vial, and it floated away from her. Then it hung in the air, unmoving.

"The Beast is still alive!" a panicked voice cried from across the square. "I can see it moving inside the barn."

Still the potion hung in the air. "Well, what are you waiting for?" Petra said.

"If I pour this on the Beast," Tom answered, "will it reverse the

animation spell and turn it back into a fang?"

Petra thought for a moment. "Maybe," she said. "But the Beast would have to swallow the potion. Someone would have to pour it right into its mouth. And you can't do that – your leg's so badly burned, I'm surprised you can even stand up!"

"I'll do it!" Elenna said.

"No!" came Tom's panicked reply. "I'd rather perish than see a hair on your head harmed."

"This is no time for jokes, Tom," Elenna said, reaching for the vial. But before she could take it, it darted away from her and bobbed unevenly across the square.

"I don't think he's joking," Petra said with a sigh, suddenly wishing she'd never set eyes on the love potion at all. *Tom really is going to get himself killed this time...*

smouldered at all. As he edged closer, Tom saw that Scalamanx's broad flank was still rising and falling. The Beast's eyes were closed, and smoke drifted up from its sleeping body.

Wincing with pain, Tom limped to the Beast's massive head to find its lips firmly closed. He glanced about for something to use as a lever and spotted a discarded broom on the floor. Tom picked it up and, barely daring to breathe, eased the broom handle between Scalamanx's teeth. An overpowering smell of ashes hit him as he prised the Beast's jaws open. The stench made him gasp and his eyes smarted with the acrid fumes. Sheathing his sword, he unstoppered the vial.

As the cork came free with a pop,
Tom saw the Beast's huge eye snap
open. It was glassy and black now,
instead of swirling orange, but
with a faint red glimmer inside. *I'm
invisible!* Tom reminded himself,
dragging his injured body closer. But

then he froze, his heart in his throat. He could see his own reflection in the dark orb of the creature's eye. *The potion has worn off!* he realised, just as the faint light in Scalamanx's iris flared bright, and its tentacles sizzled to life once more with a *whoosh*!

Tom stumbled back as the Beast's flaming whips lashed towards him, but his injured foot struck something in his path and his leg gave way. He hit the ground awkwardly and the vial rolled from his hand, its precious contents spilling across the floor.

Tom felt a rush of terror as Scalamanx heaved itself up, the lava veins that flowed beneath its scales pulsing with new light and its eyes alight with fury. Tom got to his feet and drew his sword. He could already feel the heat radiating from the Beast.

A tentacle cracked towards him. Tom swiped with his blade, severing it. Another flaming lash struck out, and Tom chopped it in half. Then another. But even as he slashed and sliced he could see the tentacles regrowing, and he could hear the crackle of flames all around him.

Choking smoke billowed through the barn, filling his lungs and blurring his vision. He glanced back to see the outline of the hay bales, now ablaze. He swung his sword blindly through the smoke, one sleeve over his mouth and nose, desperately trying to drive the Beast back.

Suddenly Scalamanx lifted its

colossal tail and sent it crashing into a row of animal stalls. Tom threw his shield above his head as the structure came tumbling down. A heavy beam struck the surface, smashing him to his knees. He tried to stand but his whole body felt heavy and weak.

The floor seemed to lurch, and his head spun, his breath rasping in his chest. He coughed, but couldn't get enough air. He found himself sinking into darkness, sagging towards the ground. He looked up, but the flames and smoke surrounding him dissolved into swimming blackness. *I'm going to pass out...* he realised. *And I didn't even get to say goodbye to Elenna...*

As the darkness fell, a memory returned to him – the Locksmith's cart

smashing into the square with Petra
on board. An idea struck him – too
late! Suddenly, he knew how to defeat
the Beast and save Elenna. But now
she would perish...

And it's all my fault.

THE BURNING BARN

Smoke poured from the roof and walls of the barn, stinging Petra's eyes. Even outside, the heat felt unbearable.

Elenna stared in horror as flames licked up through the roof. "If Tom's still in there, he'll burn to death!" she said.

"He's probably escaped, we just

can't see him because of my spell, that's all," Petra told her, trying to believe her own words. But just then a deafening roar of flames erupted inside the barn, sending sparks into the sky. A moment later Scalamanx lumbered out, its blazing eyes scanning the square and the fiery tongues around its neck crackling with new energy.

"Tom!" Elenna screamed. A group of villagers with buckets rushed towards the Beast. Scalamanx let out a hiss and reared back, its orange eyes suddenly wary. But there was still no sign of Tom. Petra cursed under her breath, then shrugged off her cloak.

"Try and keep the Beast away from the barn," she told Elenna. Then,

before she could change her mind, she
ducked her head and ran, charging
right into the burning building.

"Tom!" she called into the thick black
smoke, but her voice came out croaky
from the fumes. She stumbled on,
nearly tripping on a wooden beam in
her path. Already she felt dizzy and
weak, but she staggered through the
semi-darkness, looking for any sign of
Tom.

Suddenly she ran into a softish
bundle on the ground, almost
toppling over it. *Tom!* The potion had
worn off, but the sight of him filled
her with alarm. His eyes were closed,
and he lay as still as a corpse. Petra
crouched over him, and gave him a
shake, but he didn't move. With a

curse, Petra grabbed him by the arm, bent her knees and heaved him over her shoulder. Staggering under his weight, Petra crouched beneath the worst of the smoke, and turned. Every muscle in her body protested, but she forced herself to put one foot in front of the other, keeping eyes on the daylight ahead.

Coughing, with flames licking all around her, Petra finally pushed out of the barn. As soon as she reached open air, she collapsed to her knees, gasping for breath. Elenna rushed to her side and eased Tom from her shoulders, lowering him to the ground. She looked stricken, her eyes wide and her face pale as ash.

"He isn't breathing," she muttered. "And I can't feel a pulse."

Petra felt sick, as if someone had punched her in the stomach. "He can't be...dead?" She knew how to heal cuts and burns. But she couldn't raise the dead.

Elenna didn't answer. Instead, with a look of grim determination, she tipped Tom's head back. Then she put her mouth over his and breathed into his lungs. A moment later, she started pumping his chest with her hands. Over and over she breathed and pumped, while Petra watched on, dimly aware of flames and smoke all around them, and the shouts of villagers as they threw water at the Beast. *Please don't die!*

Suddenly Tom took a rasping breath and coughed. Elenna propped him up with her arm as he opened his eyes and started to struggle. Relief washed over Petra and a few hot tears escaped down her cheeks.

"Tom! Are you all right?" Elenna asked.

Tom gazed up into her eyes and smiled, then lifted a shaky hand to his lips. "Thanks to you," he said. "You saved my life…" Then he took another rasping breath, and his eyes opened wide as if he'd just remembered something. "The cart!" he croaked. "The keys. Get the Locksmith's keys!"

"Why?" Petra asked. But Elenna's face brightened.

"Of course!" she said. "We need to get the Beast somewhere cold. That will slow him down." And as Elenna said the words, Petra remembered the stinging blast of snow on her face.

"I think I can help," she said. Petra turned to see a group of villagers

throwing the last of their water over
the Beast while it raged and stamped.
She set off at a run, skirting around
the edge of the smoke-filled square
until she reached the toppled cart.
The Locksmith's box had fallen
open and the keys lay scattered on
the cobbles. Petra dropped to her
knees and started scrabbling through
them, looking for one she recognised.
There! She grabbed the key, just as
a thunderous roar from the Beast
shook the ground. She glanced up
to see the villagers scattering, their
buckets empty. Scalamanx's lava
seams had dimmed to a smouldering
dark red, but his eyes still blazed as
he lumbered after them.

Petra leaped up to see Elenna

supporting Tom as he limped her way.

"I'm pretty sure this one leads to the Icy Plains," she told them, holding out the key.

"Perfect," Tom said, taking it. "Now we just need to get Scalamanx's attention."

"That should be easy enough," Petra said. She turned to see the Beast storming after the retreating villagers, its tentacles lank and smoking. She backed into the doorway of a nearby tavern. Tom and Elenna crowded in beside her. Then Petra muttered a spell and fired a bolt of blue magic. The Beast growled as the sizzling bolt struck its flank. Then it swung around to fix them with a furious glare.

Tom brandished his sword, and Petra hurled another bolt, hitting Scalamanx right between the eyes. With a mighty roar, the Beast lunged towards them.

"That seems to have done the trick," Petra said, as Tom fitted the key into the tavern's lock. It turned with a click, and Tom thrust the door open.

A sharp, icy wind slammed into Petra as she bundled through after Tom and Elenna. Her feet sank deep into powdery snow. Tom and Elenna staggered ahead of her down a steep snow dune. Petra scrambled after them, already shivering, the piercing cold chilling her to the bone. Suddenly, she heard a hiss of fury and turned. The Beast stood at the

top of the slope, black and smoking
against the snowy landscape, but
with eyes as red as burning coals.
Petra swallowed. From the hatred in
Scalamanx's gaze, she could tell it
was ready to fight to the death.

ON THE ICY PLAINS

Elenna took Tom's arm, pulling him onwards down the snowy slope, away from the open door where the Beast slunk through, his red eyes filled with hatred. *So far so good*, Tom thought as he limped after his friend, the freezing wind buffeting him from every direction. When they reached the bottom of the dune, they stepped out on to the icy surface of a lake. Tom felt his feet slipping in different directions, and Elenna almost fell as she struggled to help him. Somehow, they got their footing and turned.

"What now?" asked Petra, skidding alongside them.

Looking back up at the Beast, Tom could see Scalamanx's movements slowing, most of its body completely black with only a few streaks of deep red left. The door to Rion was still open, the key in the lock, and Tom could see the daylight beyond.

"We should slip around the Beast and close the door!" Elenna cried over the wind. "If we trap Scalamanx here, it'll soon freeze completely. Petra – you head right, I'll go left. That way at least one of us should make it."

"I don't much like those odds, but I'll take any chance to get out of this wind!" Petra answered.

"Go!" Tom said. "I'll keep the Beast busy until you're through." As the girls struck off up the slope at opposite angles, their heads bent into the wind, Tom drew his sword and grabbed his shield. Then he crouched down, ready to fight. His teeth chattered and his hands shook, but he could see Elenna ploughing through the snow to safety, and the sight gave him all the strength he needed.

Scalamanx padded towards Tom, steam hissing up from the snow all around. Giving a roar, the Beast lashed out with one of its

smouldering tentacles. Tom sliced
with his sword, lopping it off. Another
tentacle whipped towards him, slower
than before. Tom made a strike for it
with his blade, but his arm felt stiff
and clumsy, the muscles frozen. He

managed to block the tentacle just a fraction from his face. *Chop!* The severed tentacle fell, sending up a hiss of steam as it hit the ice. No new tentacle grew to take its place.

It's working! Tom realised. *The cold is draining Scalamanx's strength!* He glanced up to see Elenna nearing the portal. *Once she's safe, I'll run for it.*

Tom took a few skidding steps backwards over the frozen lake. The Beast trudged after him with jerky, clumsy steps, its feet sinking into the ice with a hiss. Dark water welled up, making plumes of steam, but still Scalamanx ploughed onwards.

It's nearly defeated, Tom thought, readying himself to race past the cooling lava Beast. *Any second now…*

But suddenly Scalamanx raised its colossal tail high, then let it fall with a mighty *BOOM!* The ice bucked, throwing Tom from his feet. Clods of snow slammed into his face and chest, blinding him and shocking him with sudden cold. As he cleared his eyes and clambered up, a giant foreleg kicked him right in the chest, sending him skidding backwards over the ice. At the top of the dune, Tom could see Petra and Elenna right by the door.

"Go!" he cried.

Elenna shook her head. "Not without you!" Tom felt a rush of gratitude. He drew on the last of his strength. *I can't let her down!* A moment later, Petra grabbed Elenna's hand and stepped through the door, yanking Elenna with her.

Slowly, painfully, Tom got to his feet and brandished his sword. Scalamanx growled, sending puffs of yellow smoke into the freezing air, then heaved itself onwards through the ice. One enormous foot plunged through the frozen lake's surface, then another. Water oozed out, sending up more steam. The Beast gave a hideous roar and shuddered. Another foot disappeared through the ice as it tried to struggle free.

It's now or never... Tom took his chance and ran. Wind howled in his ears and he couldn't feel his frozen feet as he skidded over the ice, past the Beast, then pounded up the snowy slope. The door to Rion was almost in reach. Tom forced his numb legs to carry him the last few steps. He could see Elenna beckoning frantically.

BANG! The door slammed shut in his face, caught by a sudden gust. *No!* Tom's heart gave a painful lurch. As the door vanished, his injured foot twisted beneath him. He toppled and started to slide back towards the lake. Frozen to the bone, and with the last of his strength spent, he couldn't stop himself. He slipped and tumbled right down the dune, then staggered up, dizzy and shuddering with cold, to find himself staring into the Beast's glassy eyes. They were almost black, with only the faintest glimmer inside. Shivering uncontrollably, his body numb almost to the core, Tom lifted his sword, just as the Beast swung its tail. Tom saw it coming, but his trembling muscles wouldn't react. The tail lashed his feet out from under him. He hit the ice, his sword spinning away, to see Scalamanx's open jaws right above him.

1

7

THE LOVE POTION

Tom shut his eyes, waiting for the
explosion of agony that would come
as the Beast's massive jaws closed
over his head. But no pain came. The
smell of ash filled his nostrils. He
opened his eyes a crack to see the
dark insides of the salamander's vast
maw. But the Beast wasn't moving. *It's
frozen!* Tom realised.

Tom wriggled downwards over the

ice, freeing himself, then retrieved his sword and struggled to his feet. The wind scoured the deserted landscape, and Tom hugged his freezing body as he stared at the Beast. Scalamanx's scales and flesh had turned

completely black. Its eyes were open, but dark and lifeless, like volcanic glass. *It's a statue – nothing more. But I'm still trapped here, alone.* Tom sat down with a thump, his body feeling suddenly, strangely warm. *At least Elenna's safe...* he thought. But his eyelids drooped. *I'm so very tired...*

"Tom!" Elenna's voice reached him over the wind. He forced his eyes open and looked up the dune to see Elenna and Petra stepping through the door to Rion. He tried to stand, but his legs were heavy as lead. He couldn't move.

Petra and Elenna started through the snow towards him. He felt a jolt of pain as each took one of his arms, then heaved him to his feet.

Between them, they half-dragged and half-carried him over the ice and up the slope, grabbing his sword as they passed it.

Petra and Elenna helped Tom through the door and out into the warmth of a summer's day. A terrific cheer went up, and Tom glanced about to see the square filled with smiling villagers, and most of the fires already out. It felt unreal, when just a moment before he'd been freezing to death with his head in the jaws of the Beast.

"Are you all right?" Elenna asked. Tom's leg was in agony, and he could feel the sharp pain of deep burns on his back. His lungs ached and his eyes felt dry and gritty. He had never felt so tired in his life. But Elenna was at his side, brave, loyal and beautiful.

He shot her a grin. "I think I need the kiss of life again," he said.

Elenna frowned, and Petra giggled.

"What's going on?" Elenna demanded, turning on the witch. But Petra just held up her hands.

"I know nothing," she said, "but don't you think you had better shut that door?"

Elenna scowled at her but pulled the door to the Icy Plains shut with a bang then took the key from the lock. "As long as this key is kept safe, Scalamanx will never trouble anyone again," she said.

Tom let himself sag gratefully against Elenna's shoulder. *Our Quest is done!*

Two days later, an anxious Elenna stood by Tom's bed in the infirmary. Tom watched Daltec give the cup of smoking liquid in his hand a final stir.

"I hope this works," Elenna said as Daltec held the cup out towards Tom.

"Drink this," Daltec said. "It will reverse any enchantments you've been under." With his burns healing, and his strength returning hour by hour, Tom had never felt better.

"But I'm fine," he said.

Daltec raised an eyebrow. "Then the potion won't need to do anything," he said. "Please just trust me."

Tom frowned down at the stinking liquid, then up at Elenna. She was

watching him, her eyes full of worry.
If it will make my beloved happy…
Tom took a deep breath, put the
cup to his lips and took a sip. The

liquid trickled down his throat like fire. Then all at once, terrible heat spread outwards from his stomach – it felt like a deep, burning shame. He blushed as he remembered suddenly how he'd been acting towards Elenna – how her every movement had filled him with wonder and joy.

"How do you feel now?" she asked him, frowning slightly.

"I... I..." Tom could barely bring himself to speak as memories swirled in his mind. "I'm so sorry... I don't know what came over me. I need to apologise for my behaviour. I have never... You're my friend. A brave, true friend, but I don't think of you as a... Not that you aren't beautiful, of course..." Tom stopped, suddenly realising he was babbling.

"It's all right, Tom," Elenna said, grinning with what looked like relief. "You were under an enchantment."

"But how?" Tom asked.

"Take a guess," Elenna said.

Tom nodded. "Petra!" Just then the infirmary door burst open. Stefan and Sorella marched through.

"Where is the witch?" Sorella demanded.

"She fled," Daltec said. "But in recognition of her help in defeating Scalamanx, I think it's only right she goes free – after all, she didn't break into your vault. That was the Locksmith."

"And where is he?" Stefan asked.

"I'm afraid he escaped too," Tom

said, lowering his head.

"So, you've failed on all counts then?" Sorella snapped.

"Hardly!" Elenna cut in. "We defeated a Beast and returned all your stolen property. If you had taken better care of your dangerous artefacts, none of this would have happened in the first place."

Sorella glowered.

"And don't forget," Daltec said, "you promised to restore Tom's magical powers if he found the artefacts."

"Yes, yes," Sorella said crossly, waving a hand. "And the Circle of Wizards will keep its word. We have all the Locksmith's keys safely in our keeping now, so with nothing further to do here, we'll leave at once." Sorella swept the room with a furious, haughty gaze, then snapped her fingers. A flash of white light filled the infirmary. When it faded, Stefan and Sorella were gone.

Daltec stepped towards Tom's bed, grinning broadly. More than grinning. He was smirking.

"What?" Tom said.

"The Circle doesn't have all the Locksmith's keys!" the young wizard said. He reached into his robe and drew out a single key. "I was able to experiment with them before I handed them over." Daltec crossed to the chamber door, slotted his key in the lock, then pulled it open. The whole room was instantly filled with the sound of birdsong and rushing waves. Through the door, Tom could see golden sands and clear blue water. And Petra, lying in a hammock strung between two palm trees. She held up a coconut shell in her hand, then took a sip from the top.

"Mmm!" she said. Then she waved back at them through the door. "You should come through," she called. "The water is lovely and warm!"

Tom swung his legs out of bed and grinned at Elenna. "What do you say?"

"Sounds good to me!" she replied.

Daltec nodded. "I think we all deserve a holiday."

They stepped together through the door. As sunshine beat down on Tom's aching body, he felt the stiffness in his muscles start to ease at once. He took

CONGRATULATIONS,
YOU HAVE COMPLETED
THIS QUEST!

At the end of each chapter you were
awarded a special gold coin.
The QUEST in this book was
worth an amazing 14 coins.

Look at the Beast Quest totem picture
opposite to see how far you've come
in your journey to become

MASTER OF THE BEASTS.

The more books you read,
the more coins you will collect!

Do you want your own
Beast Quest Totem?
1. Cut out and collect the coin below
2. Go to the Beast Quest website
3. Download and print out your totem
4. Add your coin to the totem

www.beastquest.co.uk

a deep breath, filling his lungs with fresh sea air, then dug his toes into the warm sand. *Ahhh!* he thought. *I feel better already – fit enough to start a new Quest! Well, almost...*

THE END

READ THE BOOKS, COLLECT THE COINS!
EARN COINS FOR EVERY CHAPTER YOU READ!

550+ COINS
MASTER OF
THE BEASTS

410 COINS
HERO

350 COINS
WARRIOR

230 COINS
KNIGHT

180 COINS
SQUIRE

44 COINS
PAGE

8 COINS
APPRENTICE

550+
515
480
445
410
395
380
365
350
320
290
260
230
217
206
191
180
145
112
78
44
30
19
8

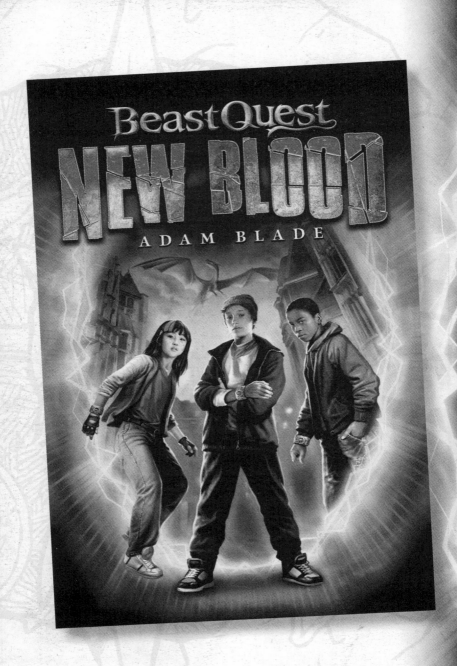

BeastQuest
NEW BLOOD
ADAM BLADE

Meet three new heroes with the power to tame the Beasts!

Amy, Charlie and Sam – three children from our world – are about to discover the powerful legacy that binds them together.

They are descendants of the *Guardians of Avantia*, an elite group of heroes trained by Tom himself.

Now the time has come for a new generation to unlock the power of the Beasts and fulfil their destiny.

BEAST QUEST

ULTIMATE HEROES

Find out more about
the NEW mobile game at
www.beast-quest.com